"When we do the best that we can, we never know what miracle is wrought in our life, or in the life of another."

— *Helen Keller*

RAINBOWS
in the dark

By Jan Coates

Illustrated by Alice Priestley

Second
Story
Press

"Second Time Around stinks!" Abby glared at her mom and slammed the car door – hard!

"Maybe there'll be other kids there today," Mom said, smiling. She headed straight for "Men's Pants," leaving Abby staring sullenly at the unappealing pile of toys spilling out of a laundry basket. She threw herself into the pink stuffed chair, crossed her arms and scowled.

The door suddenly banged open and a blast of cold air swept a young woman into the store. Laughing, she struggled to push her hair back from her face.

*A*bby came up out of her slump. The woman held a weird-looking leash. The leash was hooked to a white leather harness. And inside the harness was a big chocolate-brown dog. Didn't the woman see the sign? It clearly said, "No Dogs Allowed!"

Abby inched her way closer as the stranger sifted through the bins of "Women's Blouses," humming to herself. The dog sniffed curiously as Abby approached.

"Excuse me?" she began, clearing her throat. "But dogs aren't supposed to be here — in case you didn't know," she finished, her voice trailing off.

The woman jumped slightly, then giggled. "Thanks for the tip, but Charlie isn't just any dog — he's working right now, believe it or not!"

"Dogs don't work – they're too lazy!" Abby scoffed.

"Charlie's different – he's a guide dog. He helps me get around, because I can't see," the woman explained.

"Oh," Abby said in a small voice, staring at the floor. "How come you're wearing sunglasses?"

"It's more comfortable for me," the woman replied.

Abby reached out to pat Charlie. The dog began to pant. His teeth were enormous! "Does he bite?" she asked, stepping back.

"No, but please don't pet him or anything when he's working," the woman said quietly. "Charlie needs to focus to help me find cross-walks and stairs and doors – he keeps me safe. He's such a good worker, even squirrels can't distract him!"

"Oh," Abby said, edging closer. "But doesn't he ever get to play?"

"Sure he does – when we're at home and he's off-duty. Charlie's my very best friend!"

"Hey – he's smiling!" Abby interrupted.

The woman laughed. "I'm Joanna, by the way. You know what? I could use your help too – if you're not busy, that is?"

"I'm Abby and I'm sooooo bored! That's my mom over there," Abby said, waving. "Oh … I guess you can't see her, though," she mumbled.

"That's okay. Here's my problem. Even though Charlie is the best friend anyone could ask for, he's no help with colors. Dogs see everything in black and white. Could you help me pick out some clothes?"

Abby bobbed her head up and down. "I know lots of colors – my Mom's a painter, and we have zillions of paint tubes at home in tons of colors!"

"How wonderful!" Joanna smiled, plunging her hands back into the bin. "I need a very special outfit. Something nice, but not too frilly." She untangled a blouse from the bright clouds of silk and satin. "This feels lovely. What does it look like?"

Abby hesitated, then decided to be honest. "It's kind of like dirty snow – the kind Mom says not to eat. It's not very pretty, I don't think."

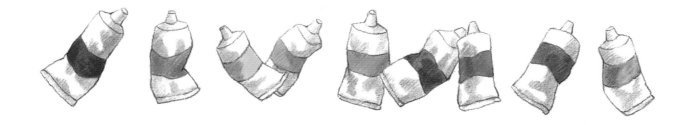

Rummaging in the bin, Abby pulled out another shirt. "How does this one feel?" she asked.

Joanna held it up to her cheek. "Mmmmm – very nice – like a cool ocean breeze!"

"It's purple!" Abby said excitedly. "My best color – like those tiny spring flowers, ummmm...."

"Violets!" Joanna said. "Like the purple in rainbows. I miss rainbows so much...." Charlie gave a big sigh, and nudged her with his nose.

Abby frowned. "I wished for a hundred rainbows once, for my birthday – when I was really little. Isn't that dumb?"

"There's no harm in wishing for magic," Joanna replied. "I do it all the time."

*C*hoosing a skirt was even more of a challenge. "Too squiggly," "too mustardy," "too yucky," Abby declared, groaning. "Too short, too tight!" Joanna added. Finally she held a flowing skirt up to her waist.

"How about this?" she asked.

Abby clapped her hands. "I love it! It's blue and black – all mixed up. Like the sky when we go camping and the moon is hiding. It even has tiny stars! I wish it fit me!" Into the basket it swished, nestling next to the violet blouse.

"Follow me to the shoes," Abby commanded, skipping ahead. "Oops!" she said, remembering – but it was okay, Charlie was leading Joanna across the room.

"Cinderella shoes!" Abby exclaimed, picking up a sparkly silver pair and trying one on.

Joanna felt them carefully. "Ankle-breakers!" she pronounced.

"Too small," "too ugly," "too slippery." About to give up, Abby suddenly squealed with delight.

"Awesome! These just have to fit! They're like peacock feathers – all green and purple and gold and black." Joanna tried the right shoe and smiled. She tried the left one....

"Absolutely perfect!" she said, taking a few steps. "I think I'm all set!"

"What about jewels?" Abby reminded her, picking through a jumble of glitter. "Oh, Joanna! Here – feel how velvety. It's purpley-black – like a fuzzy plum. And there's a bunch of diamonds – well, they're probably fake – and a skinny moon. Why would anybody ever give this away?"

And there was Joanna, perched on a chair in the very center of the stage. The night-sky skirt flowed around her cello; the peacock shoes peeked out between the folds. A full orchestra filled the stage behind her. Charlie sat quietly by her side.

Abby clapped her hands and jumped up and down. "She's the star, Mommy, isn't she? Why is her fiddle so big? She looks like a princess. And Charlie's so handsome!"

Then Joanna began to play, her elegant arms and hands weaving back and forth across the strings. A bewitching mix of music and color billowed up, filling every corner of the enormous concert hall.

$\mathcal{A}$s Joanna played, a brilliant beam of moonlight shone through the rain-splattered windows. Abby caught a flicker of movement out of the corner of one eye. Glancing up at the chandelier, she gasped. A kaleidoscope of color; tiny perfect rainbows shimmered up and down the walls and skipped across the ceiling.

Abby reached for her mom's hand and snuggled into her shoulder. "Oh, Mom …" she breathed. "It's my wish! It's magic! Joanna's making the rainbows dance – just for us!"

This book is for my parents, who are always with me, and for my first readers, Don, Liam and Shannon, with love.
— J.L.C.

For Elisabeth and Voula.
— A.P.

Library and Archives Canada Cataloguing in Publication

Coates, Jan, 1960-
Rainbows in the dark / written by Jan Coates ; illustrated by Alice Priestley.

ISBN 1-896764-95-9

1. Blind--Juvenile fiction. 2. Picture books for children. I. Priestley, Alice II. Title.

PS8605.O238R33 2005   jC813'.6   C2005-903124-7

Text copyright © 2005 by Jan Coates
Illustrations copyright © 2005 by Alice Priestley
First published in the USA in 2006

Designed by P. Rutter

Special thanks to the Helen Keller Foundation and Keller Johnson Thompson for use of the quotation by Helen Keller.

Second Story Press gratefully acknowledges the support of the Ontario Arts Council and the Canada Council for the Arts for our publishing program. We acknowledge the financial support of the Government of Canada through the Book Publishing Industry Development Program, and the Government of Ontario through the Ontario Media Development Corporation's Ontario Book Initiative.

ONTARIO ARTS COUNCIL
CONSEIL DES ARTS DE L'ONTARIO

Canada Council
for the Arts

Conseil des Arts
du Canada

Published by:
SECOND STORY PRESS
20 Maud Street, Suite 401
Toronto, Ontario, Canada
M5V 2M5

www.secondstorypress.ca